The Buddha The Man Who Could Not See & Short Stories & Poems

CALEB DYLAN

Copyright © 2021 Caleb Dylan

All rights reserved.

ISBN: 9798593022905

DEDICATION

To Tammy.
My wife, my teacher, my inspiration.

CONTENTS

	Acknowledgments	i
1	The Old Man Who Could Not See	2
2	The Silent Man	7
3	The Dying Man	12
4	The Sad Jester	18
5	The Girl Who Was Bullied	23
6	The Swallowtail	28
7	The Birthday Cake	33
8	The Greedy Kingfisher	36
9	The Wise Moon	38
10	Angel	40
11.	A Selection of Poems by Caleb Dylan.	

ACKNOWLEDGMENTS

A special thankyou to the following.

Tammy, Sophie, Robert, Caleb, Dylan, Jack, Connor, Nevaeh, Archie,
&
Willow.

THE LAUGHING BUDDHA & OTHER STORIES

THE LAUGHING BUDDHA & THE MAN WHO COULD NOT SEE

Once upon a time, there lived an old man who was blind. He had never been able to see, and he was sad because all his friends could see, but he could not.

One day, he decided to go and talk to the Laughing Buddha. He had been told of The Buddhas great magical powers. He wondered if the Laughing Buddha would be able to make him see. So, he set off on the long journey, across rivers, forests, mountains, and plains. The journey was long, and it took the old man many days and nights. Finally, very tired, he found the Laughing Buddha sitting under the old Bodhi tree.

"Hello" said the Laughing Buddha, "you look very tired and hungry old man, is there some way that I can help you?"

"Oh yes" replied the old man. "Where I come from, I have many friends, who have told me that you have magical powers, and that, if I come to talk to you, you will be able to give me light". To this, the Buddha started to laugh. He laughed and laughed. The old man thought this was rather rude, and asked the Laughing Buddha "why do you laugh so? is the fact I am blind something you find funny?"

"Oh no" said the Laughing Buddha. It's just that you have asked me to give you light when you have the power of vision already". "How is this so?" came the reply.

"Old man, on your journey here, did you cross the River of Eternity?" "Yes" said the old man. "Well, how did you know you were there?".

"Why I heard the fish jumping upstream, amongst the babbling waters, that is how I know".

The Buddha asked, "On your journey here, did you travel through the Forest of Rajgir?" "Yes" replied the old man. "Well, how did you know you were there?" said Laughing Buddha. "Because I heard the trees rustling, and the Woodlark's song told me I was there".

The Buddha then asked, "On your journey here, did you cross the Mountain of Youthfulness?" "Yes" again came the reply. "So" said Buddha, "how did you know this?" "Because", said the old man, the sun's rays warmed me, and the Buzzards mew guided me".

The Buddha then asked, "On your journey here, did you cross the Great Plains of Kushinagar"? "Why yes" said the old man.

"Well, how did you know?" asked Buddha. "Because I could smell the fragrance of the Meadowsweet, and I could feel the grazing of the Great Herds".

"Finally, asked the Buddha, "how did you find me and the old Bodhi Tree?" "Why, I could smell the Sandalwood you were burning, and I could hear your laughter". "That is wonderful" said Buddha.

"You have heard the jumping fish, and the babbling waters, you have felt the warmth of the sun, and heard the buzzards mew. You have listened to the Woodlark, and the trees swaying in the gentle breeze. You have smelled the Meadowsweet and felt the grazing of great herds. Why is it you tell me you cannot see? Please listen to this proverb, and you will understand."

"There are those who drink, but do not taste.

Those who hear, but do not listen.

Those who touch, but do not feel.

And there are those who look, but do not see".

With this, the old man left the Laughing Buddha. He set off back home, on the same journey that brought him to the old Bodhi tree.

Happy in the knowledge with what the Laughing Buddha had taught him.

He was the light.

THE LAUGHING BUDDHA
&
THE SILENT MAN

Once, a long time ago in the village of Bagaha, lived a man named Mounesh.

Mounesh could not speak. Try as he may, words would not flow from his mouth. Wherever he went, people would laugh and mock him. This made Mounesh very sad indeed.

One sunny morning he decided that he would visit the Laughing Buddha. It was a long journey, and Mounesh set off in the hope that the Buddha would be able to help him to speak.

After a few miles he reached the village of Ramnagar. Here, he saw a young girl crying. As Mounesh got closer, he realized that she had grazed her knee.

Mounesh tapped her on the shoulder, and pointed to her knee, gesturing that he could help. He then pulled out a handkerchief from his pocket. Mounesh then walked over a nearby stream and dipped the handkerchief in. He walked back to the girl, and gently placed the cold, wet handkerchief on her graze. Immediately the girl was relieved. She smiled, said thank you and ran back towards her home. She turned and waved as Mounesh set off to complete his journey.

After walking several miles, Mounesh smelled smoke, then caught sight of a fire in the distance. It was a barn, and it was full of animals such as sheep and goats. None of the villagers or farmers knew there was fire raging. Mounesh saw a church, and he ran to the tower to ring the bell. He rang and rang the bell. The villagers all heard the bell and saw the fire. They quickly got to work extinguishing the fire and rescuing the animals. All the Goats and Sheep were saved. Mounesh turned to look back at the smoldering barn before continuing his journey.

That night he found a comfortable spot under a tree to rest. He thought about the day's events and drifted off to sleep. Suddenly he awoke, screaming silently. A nightmare had consumed him. He dreamt of a young boy who was drowning. Mounesh was frantically trying to shout for help, but the longer it went on, the worse the situation became for the drowning boy. He made the decision to jump in and rescue the boy, knowing he himself could not swim. As he grabbed the boy, Mounesh grabbed an overhanging branch and handed it to the boy. The boy was able to hang on until help arrived. However, Mounesh was swept away by the raging current and was lost in its depths.

Such a dream had made Mounesh feel

uncomfortable, and even more desperate to see the Laughing Buddha, to ask for help in talking.

After travelling more miles, he suddenly became aware to the smell of burning sandalwood. He could also make out the silhouette of a larger-than-life figure sitting beneath a tree. Finally, he had reached the Laughing Buddha.

"Hello Mounesh" said the Laughing Buddha, "please sit down. Would you like some tea?" Being eager to ask the Buddha about his wishes, he shook his head.

Buddha knew the man was unable to talk, but he knew why he was there.

"Mounesh" said Buddha, "I know what it is you want to ask me. I and realise how desperately you wish to speak. However, although it is not within my power to grant your wish, I have seen your journey here, and the things you have done are wonderful. Your kindness, your initiative and courage have all been given without a thought for yourself. The girl you helped in Ramnagar, her knee is now healed, and she is so happy to be without pain.

Thanks to your quick thinking, all the animals in the barn survived. And do you remember the dream you had? Well, I sent that to you. I saw your selfless courage. You saved the boy, without a thought for yourself. You were washed away downstream and would not have survived.

Mounesh, all these things showed you that the ability to talk is secondary when love, courage and selflessness are within your heart. Because you always think of others, you have not really found a need to concentrate on talking. Do you understand Mounesh"?

Mounesh said "Yes, I do."

He was healed.

THE LAUGHING BUDDHA

&

THE DYING MAN

Many decades ago, in a village called Patna, lived an old man called Sharad.

Sharad was old and very ill. Sadly, he was dying. This was something that pained Sharad very much. He did not want to die. So, he visited every Physician in Northern India to search for a cure. Each Doctor he saw was unable to help him. He was desperate. I know, he thought to himself, I will have to go and find the Laughing Buddha. He will cure me!

The next morning, he set off on the long journey to find Laughing Buddha. It was to be a long, arduous journey, and Sharad did not know if he would have the energy to make it. Nevertheless, determined, he wasted no more time.

After a few days of travelling, Sharad set up camp near an old Copper Mine. Sharad was tired, and as he lay down, a sign caught his eye. It was above a door to a mine shaft. On the sign were the words "Danger, Do Not Enter!" well, thought Sharad, I certainly have no plans to go in there! He drifted off to sleep.

The next morning when he awoke, he sipped his tea, packed his rucksack and carried on with his journey. As he continued his journey, in the distance, he could hear a running stream. Being thirsty, this sound was welcome. He bent down to drink from the stream, and as he sipped, he saw his reflection in the water. It seemed to be jumping around with the bubbling of the water. Sharad thought this was quite funny as he himself could not move that quickly, but then suddenly, he could not see his reflection anymore. The clouds above had now changed, and the reflection disappeared as the water became dark.

Sharad shivered, stood up and wandered off. As he walked, the moon became full and lit the whole sky. Sharad gazed in wonder and whispered "thank you" to the moon. It had melted the darkness away, making his journey much easier. He began to remember a song from his childhood, and he started to hum. The song was about spring, summer, autumn and winter. The words were;

'In joy we welcome the bursting spring,
Where Mother Nature's blossoms sing

To welcome summers evensong
And serenade the days so long.

In changing light, we gaze aloft.
As colours turn to meet the frost

We kneel towards the frozen moon.
And pray for springs melodic tune."

As the sun rose the following morning, Sharad

woke to the smell of Sandalwood. Something stirred inside him. He knew this meant only one thing. Sharad stood up, and over the brow of the hill he caught the sillhouette of a large man, seated beneath a tree. Incense was burning and filling the air with tranquility. He headed over to the figure, and as he gently approached a booming voice exclaimed "I've been waiting for you Sharad".

Sharad replied "How can this be? You really do have magical powers!"

"Oh, I am not so sure about that. Please take a seat".

As Sharad sat, he cleared his throat. "Sir," he started to speak. Before he could complete a sentence the Laughing Buddha said "I know what it is you want to ask of me. Before you do, I want you to consider a few things."

Buddha went on. " Sharad, I have witnessed your ponderings on your way to me." He asked "Do you remember the Copper Mine you camped near? Well, a few years ago, many lives were lost in the mine. It collapsed and fathers, brothers, uncles, sons and friends all perished."

"Your reflection in the river was short lived was it not? There one second, and gone the next?
"Yes it was" replied Sharad.
"And the moon?" Was it not beautiful that thoughtful night"?
Sharad said "Such a wonderful sight".
Buddha asked "Was the moon in the sky the following evening, or the evening after that?"
"Unfortunatley it was not" said Sharad.
Finally, Buddha said; " These things are constant reminders of impermanence. Lives of our loved ones, the ocean tides, the falling rains and the seasons you sang about. Nothing my friend, lasts forever. So you see, I know your heart is heavy at your impending death. But please remember that we are as temporary as sands in the wind. There is nothing I, or anyone can do.

All Things Must Pass".

THE LAUGHING BUDDHA & THE SAD JESTER

A long time ago, there lived a Jester. He was a very funny man, who would always make people laugh. He could juggle balls, do hand stands and was a very good dancer. But even though he could do such things, inside himself he was sad. He thought, I spend most of my time making people laugh, but no one tries to make me happy. He despaired, until one day he decided to go and find the Laughing Buddha. Surely, he would be able to make the Sad Jester happy inside?

So, the next morning he set off. He knew it would be a long and difficult journey. On the first night, he set up his hammock amongst some trees, and settled down for the evening. It was a clear starry night and the Sad Jester lay on his bed gazing up at the stars. Occasionally there would be a shooting star. So, he made a wish. He said to himself "I wish for The Laughing Buddha to make me happy. For always". He drifted off to sleep with a smile on his face. He had not felt like that for a while. In the morning he set off again, reaching a small village. He saw an old woman walking along and asked her "Excuse me, do you know which way to the Laughing Buddha?"

She replied "Many miles from here sir. No one really knows the way. It is said that if you are destined to meet him then you will find him. When you hear his chuckle, and smell Sandalwood then you have arrived. Good luck!"

"Thank you".

As he turned, he could not help noticing a little girl, sitting down, looking unhappy. "Little girl, whatever is wrong."

She replied "Oh I have hurt my foot and I cannot dance. I love to dance every day, and it makes my mother feel better. She is really sick, and it is the only thing that keeps her smiling."

"Oh dear. Perhaps I can dance for her today. Then tomorrow when your leg is feeling better, you can. Do you live in the village?"

"Oh yes" she replied. "On the farm".

"Well, let's go" he replied.

The Sad Jester danced for the girl's mother, who sat up in bed. She clapped and smiled and laughed. All the animals on the farm heard the laughter and came into the house. Goats, sheep, a cow and some chickens. There was a real commotion. Everyone laughed and laughed and laughed, until the sun went down.

A few days later, the Sad Jester came to a river. It was a welcome sight as he needed to wash and have a drink. On the riverbank was a boy, sitting quietly, his head down.

"Hello" said the Sad Jester. The boy did not reply. The boy looked upset.

The Sad Jester said again "Hello, are you alright? You look sad."

The boy replied, "My father wants me to catch the Catfish on the river bed, but I cannot swim".

"Oh dear" said the Sad Jester. "They are difficult to catch. You have to swim to the bottom and be very swift."

The boy asked, "Have you ever caught anything while fishing?"

"Well, not exactly" came the reply. "The only thing I caught was a fever!"

The boy burst out laughing. He laughed so much that he fell in the river. Before the Sad Jester had time to react, the boy was shouting "I can swim! I can swim!"

What a miracle this was. The boy felt so good, he dived. The next thing, his head was bobbing up on to the surface. He was breathless. But he was holding a small fish. "My father will be so proud. I am so happy. Thankyou sir" said the boy. The Sad Jester said, "you are welcome young man" and carried on with his journey.

The following morning the Sad Jester walked over a hill, and in the distance, he could see a figure seated beneath a tree. He could also hear laughter. Rising from the ground was a little smoke, and there was a delightful smell……sandalwood. The Sad Jester knew immediately where he was, and he was excited.

When he reached the tree, The Laughing Buddha looked up and said, "I think you must feel happy within now, Jester?"

"Why Sir, yes indeed I do. But how could you possibly know that I was unhappy in the first place?"

Buddha replied "Jester, I have seen your wondrous journey here. The happiness and relief you have brought to people has been wonderful. You truly are an inspiration for happiness. How can you possibly be sad?" The Jester was no longer The Sad Jester. He had realized that he was meant to find The Laughing Buddha, and that his journey was just a lesson sent from him.

THE LAUGHING BUDDHA
&
THE GIRL WHO WAS BULLIED

Once upon a time there was a young girl who was very sad. Every day that she went to school the other children would pick on her because she was beautiful, and the bullies were very jealous.

This made the young girl cry herself to sleep every night.

One sunny morning she decided to go and see the Laughing Buddha to see if he could help her.

She travelled many miles and slept in the

wilderness for many nights. This made her very scared, but she was so determined to see the Laughing Buddha.

On a hot sunny morning she wandered over a hill and smelled the sandalwood of the Laughing Buddha. She became excited and soon she caught sight of him sitting beneath the Bodhi Tree.

As soon as the Laughing Buddha saw the young girl, he immediately said, "hello young lady, how are you today?

"You look ready to burst with what you need to tell me". The young girl smiled and said "oh dear Laughing Buddha I so need your help. I am so unhappy and no- one, but you can help me."

"This I know" said Laughing Buddha. "I have seen with my mind's eye all that has happened to you, and I have been expecting to see you."

The girl replied "oh my goodness. I knew you had

powers but had no idea you could see things in your mind from far away."

"Ah yes" he replied. "I can only see things that I am guided to. Your need for help and your belief helped me to see what was happening. This also makes me sad. I cannot help you directly with actions, but perhaps these words will help."

"Bullies often pick on people they envy.

They are consumed with jealousy

They do not realise the hurt that they create because they have no idea of real love because they have never been shown.

It is plain to see your inner beauty, and such radiance shines despite your sadness. The bullies do not shine, as darkness is their only guide. Their lives are surrounded in negativity, therefore they become desperate for happiness. They believe that pleasing their friends and acting nastily is a good thing. Of course, you do not need me to tell you that it is not a good thing."

The girl started to cry, and immediately felt empathy for her bullies. This said the Laughing Buddha is called compassion. Not everyone has this. It is rare and compassion shows us the way we all should be.

After a cup of tea, the young girl stood up to return home. But before she did, she left these words for the Laughing Buddha;

"Laughing Buddha you have made me feel much better, and I feel much stronger to face the bullies. To know what their inner thoughts must be sad. This of course is no excuse to hurt others, but perhaps one day they will see the error of their ways and begin to feel compassion themselves. In the meantime, I will pray for them. Thank you,

Laughing Buddha."

For once the Laughing Buddha had big old tears in his eyes. He had met a young lady who had as much vision as he. He felt very humble to have been in her presence.

The Laughing Buddha continued to watch the young girl from afar.

Indeed she grew into a beautiful wise woman and lived a very long and happy life. As for the bullies...............

Karma visited them and showed them the way to feel compassion.

THE SWALLOWTAIL

A Fable of Impermanence and Attachment.

Once upon a time in the foothills of the Himalayas lived a young girl, Prisha. Prisha lived in a beautiful little house with her parents. Her life was idyllic. She lived in a wondrous place with streams and meadows. Although she had no human friends, she was never lonely, as all the animals loved her. Each morning the sheep would come to graze, and as they passed Prishas house they would bleat to say hello. Prisha would always go and sing to them whilst rubbing their necks.

Swallowtail Butterflies would sit on her shoulders to soak up the sun. Often, Prisha would go walking in the foothills. She would feed the Snow Leopard that lived there. She was not afraid as the beast never harmed her. In fact, the snow leopard would lick her and rub her fur against Prisha. The little girl's life was bliss.

 One day after a long walk, she returned home to find her father crying. He had received message that his mother was sick and dying. She needed looking after and that the family would need to move from their home to go and live with her. Prishas grandmother lived in the city, which was a long way from the mountain paradise. Prisha was upset for her grandmother who she loved very much, and although she was heartbroken, she was upset that she had to leave all her animal friends.

 That night she packed a small bag of possessions and walked, alone, into the stillness of the night, and into the hills she loved so much.
After a few miles, in the dark, Prisha slipped, hit her head

and passed out. The next thing she knew, she was lying in a bed, and her grandmother was looking over her.

"Hello Prisha, my dear" said grandmother. "How are you feeling?"
"Grandmother?" replied Prisha "I thought you were ill and dying?"
Grandmother; "Do not concern yourself with that now. You just need to rest. I am here and will look after you".
Prisha; "Oh goodness Grandmother. I am so excited. If you are here now, and you are well again, I do not have to leave all of my animal friends"!
Grandmother; "Prisha, please do not worry your little head about these things at the moment. Listen, all your animal friends love you, as you love them. The sheep, the butterflies, the snow leopard. Indeed, it was the snow leopard that rescued you and brought you home. Your parents are downstairs and happy that you are safe. But you must remember that although you love living here

and the life that you have, sometimes we need to make change. That is what our lives are all about. You see nothing lasts forever. Ask the Swallowtail Butterfly how she came to be. She started life as a tiny egg. Stuck to the underside of a leaf. A leaf that is no more, for she has eaten it when she became a Caterpillar. She munched her way through lots and lots of leaves. She needed energy for the journey ahead. She then miraculously turned into a Chrysalis, hanging once again from a leaf. There she transformed into an adult. A Beautiful Swallowtail Butterfly.

And as for me Prisha, well I have lived many summers. Suffered many harsh winters. I have turned from a girl into a wrinkly old woman. I have changed many times in my lifetime.

Now is the Autumn of my life, and another long winter awaits".

    Prisha looked up at her grandmother as she opened Prishas hand and placed something into it.

"Now Prisha, you must rest. Close your eyes." She said. Prisha shut her eyes, and what seemed like a blink, she opened them. Her father was sitting by her bed. Grandmother was gone.

"Father where is Grandmother gone"?

Her father looked sad. "Oh, darling Prisha" he said. "I'm afraid she passed away yesterday morning while you were asleep."

Prisha: "But, but that is not possible. She was with me just a few minutes ago. I spoke with her."

Father: "Oh my dear, you must have had a dream".

Prisha; "Oh yes, that must be it."

Once father left the room, Prisha felt something in her hand. As she opened it, a Swallowtail butterfly flew out of it. It landed on her shoulder, then flew out of the window.

THE BIRTHDAY CAKE

A long time ago in a village in Northern India lived a boy, Sanjay and his mother Namita. They were extremely poor and had little. Today was Sanjay's birthday, and when he arose, he ran to his mother. "Mother, today is my birthday, are we to have a feast?"
"Why no Sanjay, we have nothing".
Sanjay was upset and stormed off. He left for school without saying goodbye to his mother.

On his walk to school, Sanjay noticed an old lady bending down picking flowers. By her side was a basket.

It was full of fruit. There were grapes, bananas, and mango. Sanjay saw the old lady was not looking and swiped the basket away. He ran and ran until he reached the forest. The sun was cutting through the canopy, and Sanjay sat beneath a tree, sunning himself and gorging on all the fruit. Then he discarded the basket and went to school.

On his journey home, Sanjay saw his cousin Naitee coming towards him. "Oh Sanjay, Happy Birthday! I am so excited for you. Your mother has sworn me to secrecy, but I am ready to burst. You see, your mother has baked a cake for you". Sanjay ran the rest of the way home until he reached the house and opened the door. The smell was lingering from the mornings cooking. Sanjay said, "Hello mother, what is that delicious smell?"

"Oh Sanjay" she replied, "I am so sorry. I have saved for many weeks to buy all the ingredients for a birthday cake for you. All your favourites like cherries, sultanas and walnuts. So, this morning I put all the ingredients in a bowl, baked them in a tin and when it was cooked, I took it from the oven. It was glorious Sanjay."

"But Mother" asked Sanjay, "why are you sad? Where is the cake?"

Mother wept and said "When the cake was cooling, there came a knock at the door. It was a little old lady. She was selling flowers. She was so sad and looked unwell. So, when I asked her why she was sad, she told me that in the morning someone had taken her basket of fruit. She told me she had saved for weeks for the fayre. So, Sanjay, I am afraid I gave her the cake" Mother continued "She looked so happy when she saw the cake. Her eyes lit up, and the tears dried. She went away with a huge smile on her face".

Sanjay was crying. He felt so bad inside. The feeling of losing out on a cake meant nothing compared to the guilt in his heart.

Namita said "She did give me a flower though. A

little sprig of Rosemary."

Sanjay asked "Mother, may I have the Rosemary, for my birthday?"

"Yes of course" she replied.

Sanjay went to his room. There he opened a book and slipped the Rosemary inside. Then closed the book. He had learnt a lesson he would never forget.

THE GREEDY KINGFISHER

Sat on a sunlit riverbank was a young Kingfisher. As he scanned the river, he noticed another Kingfisher across the way. "I am going to catch all the fish in this river!" he said to himself. "I do not want any other taking my fish!"

Suddenly like a blue flash he darted into the water and pulled out a fish. The other Kingfisher just sat and watched. The young Kingfisher dived again. Now he had two fish.

He did this again and again, until his bill could take no more fish. He thought to himself "I am the king of this river" and sat on the riverbank puffing out his chest and feeling proud. But his mouth was so full he could not swallow any of his catch. So, he dropped one.

The other Kingfisher came along and swept it up, swallowing it in one big gulp.

The young Kingfisher had to drop another fish. The same thing happened.

Again, and again the young Kingfisher had to release more fish to be able to breath.

Finally, he was left with one fish. All the others had been taken.

THE WISE MOON

Once upon a time lived an old man called Samarth.

Samarth was very lonely. He had no friends. He lived in a hut, close to the river in the Northern part of India.

Every morning Samarth would go fishing for his lunch. Then in the afternoon he would forage for berries. In the evening he would sit and ponder. On some nights the moon would be full. On one particular full moon,

Samarth looked up at the big yellow disc and said, "Why am I all alone dear Moon?". "Why does no one seek my company?". The Moon just stared back. Samarth shrugged, and as he stood up a booming voice said "What do you think I can do about it? Have you ever seen me with another moon?".

Samarth was surprised that the Moon even replied to his question. The Moon continued "Perhaps it is because you have all you will ever need. Loneliness is a choice. No one ever has to be lonely. All you have to do is look around you. Answer me this; When you are laying in your bed at night, have you noticed there is a spider above your bed? He is busy living his little life to the full. And when you scratch your head do you not feel the lice that roam your locks?

Have you ever noticed the mouse who comes out to nibble on the crumbs you leave behind?". The Moon went on; The pillow you rest your head on, do you not realise that someone, somewhere made it, with their own hands and time.

How on earth can you say you are alone?"

ANGEL

An Angel fell to earth.

Her wings were broken.

There was no-one to help the Angel until an old man came by.

"What has happened?" he asked the Angel. The Angel explained that the wind had caught them and that their wings had become entangled in the branches of a tree. The old man said, "I will help you fix them". The Angel said "Thankyou".

The old man gathered as many feathers as he could. He fetched some yarn and a needle. Soon, he was hard at work.

After a while, the old man's wife came by. "What are you doing? You should be in bed resting for you are not well". "Aah wife" replied the old man. "I just need to finish these wings and then I will rest. Have you ever known me to lie around all day doing nothing?" She replied "but the doctor has told you to rest. It could be very dangerous for you to over stretch yourself".

"Why? do you think I might die?" asked the old man. His wife wept and said, "yes dear husband."

The old man laughed, then carried on with the repairing of the wings.

Once the wings were completed, he returned the wings to the Angel. "Here you are" he said. "Now you can carry on flying around as before!"

He then said to the Angel "Do you mind if I ask you the reason you came to earth?"

"I don't mind at all. Do you not know the answer?"

She went on "I have come to collect you."

THE LAUGHING BUDDHA & OTHER STORIES

A SELECTION OF POEMS

BY

CALEB DYLAN.

THE LAUGHING BUDDHA & OTHER STORIES

Grey Sky

Grey, oh grey sky

Whose backdrop 'doth highlight the windswept

Jackdaws returning, to sleep

In woodland covens of gregarious rapture

Whose canvas conveys the greens of

Oak and Lime

In contrasting nature

Grey, oh grey sky

Whose baskets filled with winter rains

Feed the streams,

Nourish the earth

And run to the sea

To re-unite

In generous fervour

Grey, oh grey sky

Where snow laden hills hide the Mountain Hare

And Ptarmigan

From the hunters wrath

And Weasels snout

In blanketed wonder

Grey, oh grey sky

The frosts you suffocate

With your warming hands

THE LAUGHING BUDDHA & OTHER STORIES

So the Lapwings fields still nourish
In softer earth
Where Moles do blindly play
As Buzzards ponder

Grey, oh grey sky
Whose tears rain down on moorland herds
Whilst autumns gales tear limbs
Once laden
With cuckoo spit and doves scrapes
Poplars towering landscapes
Now summers murmur

In Essence

Surrounded by rapture, my sunken eyes will fuse with a burning
So bright
For Venus is beside me, to lighten my darkest night
I will dip into your pools of perfection

To swim softly in your soul

Soaked in a lovers affection

Through silken locks I stroll

Footsteps

As we meandered across those fragrant mystic hills

Minds embroiled in each other's words and more

We did gleefully join hands

And promise evermore

To journey through life's destiny

Wherever we may roam

'cross fields and towns and open seas

To find our way back home.

The Rook

In November woods

Where Bax did write

Synonymous to a garish flight

Do Rooks abound

Amidst high tales

Of swirling mists and

Autumn gales

Congealing, scheming

Rampant screaming

Liars, cheats with

No redeeming

Rooks will call eternal taunts

Until their sins

'doth leave thy daunt

The Storm

I feel battered and bruised

Lethargy has set in

And my every motion, now a misdemeanor

I have weathered months and years

Suffered loss and shed such tears

From my inner sanctum

Stripped bare, barren, leaner

As clouds gather, dark and fierce
I remember once they pierced
My fragile heart until it beat a broken rhythm
Rain did soak my driest night
Until nothing seemed quite right
Now my mind a jaded broken cataclysm.

All I Need is Thee

I will look and I will see
All that lies beyond thee
Hills that rise from valleys low
Peaks of mountains capped in snow

Clouds that weep across the lands
Sea spew ebbing on the sands
O'er moors and heaths of pheasants roam

The nest of rooks returning home

Infant lambs on ancient fields
Kicking high as nature yields
The calf and foal in spring time highs
Amidst the mystic windward sighs

Leaves bemoan the onward chill
Among the fury of their spills
As carpets lay beneath the sea
All that I ever need is thee

The Stream

I am divine

I flow like the clearest wine

Over fish and stone

'cross hills and loam

I breathe all life as I cut my way

Through the woods and meadows

Of fragrant May

In winters realm I breathe as ice

For mountains springs of which I slice

And head towards the endless sea

To begin again my life's journey.

Meadow Hymn

The Alder, whose grace 'doth wrestle with the wind

Who's streams gallop ever on

Will rejuvenate lost whims

As shadows dance before thee

And whose leaves will carpet fields

Naked from scorched earth

In summers fury

Till the cuckoo calls aloft

Your budding branches

Behold, eternal giver

Of sunlit dewy landcapes

The Crow will call once more

To take the seeds of plenty

And scatter them

Ever onwards.

THE LAUGHING BUDDHA & OTHER STORIES

The Test Way

Shall I breathe in your salty mists
And wonder through your brackish outcrops
Swooning at your sunset
Whilst ruffs and pheasants
Dance between the raindrops

Shall I tender your moistened trail
And slumber at your feet
Shimmering in half glee as
Trout and willows tremble
Where sea and fresh do meet

Where celandine can wonder free
In capsicum and rose
Of bindweed, dock and nettle
'mongst the oak leaves
Near hedgerows

Shall I breathe again in springtime
Your stillness, as I glide across in time
Rain soaked tramplings underfoot

THE LAUGHING BUDDHA & OTHER STORIES

In pools of mossy rhyme

Or dance along your footbridge
As poo sticks find their way
Long ripples swirling endlessly
Meandering, mongst the reed beds
Of dragonflies and may

 Peacocks flicker aimlessly
Gorging on the dew
Of tufted crowns and willow herb
Surrendering
Like summers last cries and hue

Shall I pass along your coppiced hides
To see the herons stilts

And taste the brackish waterways
Of curlews calls
Till winter wilts

The sun kissed irises
Snagging through the earth
Bellowing in harvest gold
As bees elbow through the thickets
Sacks sweet of nectars mirth

Shall my swan song resonate all dear
Whilst swallows chase the fly
Or magpies congregate in oak trees
Chattering like crickets
'mongst the stems of sweet July

Oh I will return in favour all I've drunk from thee
Season after season,
Like a minstrel, sewing daisy chains

Harping endlessly

In realms of calico

In a Field Amongst Cornflowers

Peering through the harvest gold, in candid splendour

A glimpse of reef and spray

Sun kissed by the ocean's hues

Deep as bottled May

THE LAUGHING BUDDHA & OTHER STORIES

The Bee returns in favour, to trample all you sow

So guided by your scented hairs

Of sentiment and bow

Autumn Sonnet

Can barren lands amidst Gods realm

Nourish with thy tiny acorns seed

Abound in natures healing grasp, and hoe

Of which we children of the earth do feed?

Are fruits in earnest bountiful, from limbs of autumns fields

Wholesome, sweet with maidens tears

Filled with sun kissed memories

In plenty as it yields?

The lamb whose stock that fills thy trough

Seasoned with the herb and bone

Does nearly taste as sweet as song

Whose folk do worship, akin their own

The Oak

Beneath the oak to settle, my cold palate, void of gods and high

Discovering your blood that runs

From the ebbing spring tide sigh

Nourish your fruits in baskets, and leaves

Covering the green until,

the autumn winds that bristle 'mongst

Your limbs no longer still
Stripped naked, stark, and barren
Once where your arms lay claim
To landscapes where your majesty
Will guard with strength again

The Owl at Midnight

Whisper
In retreat of dawn
As the moist returns to the wood
Your night beckoned as hope conquers all not good
Silent
As the spirits dance

When all around you sleep as still

As windless sycamores

On shadowless hills

Rise again when boys turn on their lamps

To tales of fear and fury 'mongst the frosted veil

And ice becomes the carpet, your wing belies the sound

Upon the voles last scratchings

In the wise forsaken ground.

Oh Blackbird

Where briars hang, whilst meadows swoon in the shying breeze

The sweetest motet serenades the murmur of the yielding trees

Amidst the moonlit canopies on the eve of wondrous light

Your harmonious cacophony

Resolutes the darkest night

As did once my heart abscond beneath a shimmering kiss

Now your melodies to which I long for

Feed my bliss

Oh Blackbird do not shy away from your immortal song

For 'tis sat beneath your velvet wings I now belong.

The Moon my Lover

Oh moon

How I envy thee

When all is flux beneath

Unyielding in its demise

I look afar to see your stillness

THE LAUGHING BUDDHA & OTHER STORIES

Your light doth banish the darkness

Oh sweet sentinel watch over me
For love doth bring such melancholy
Absorbed I am amongst your rays
Oh shine, please shine, for
I am shrouded 'neath briars that hang
Amidst your gaze

Jewel, I do love thee
For as strong as the oceans you yield
My fortitude you do feed
Unknowing whilst bestowing ardour
When all around is alight
Burning in nonchalance

Oh moon join me in this dance

As my heart 'doth pain me

For clouds do shroud your smile

Until they fade away

Growing Pains

Go climbing 'mongst loves melodies

In realms of willows, rustling in the summer breeze

Go forth to resonate the shying winds

That dance before the moonlight,

as the daylight ends

THE LAUGHING BUDDHA & OTHER STORIES

Tread shyly through the meandering fields
Where a Skylark sings a song that yields
Memories of growing pains
Whilst running free down leafy lanes
Protected by Oak canopies
We danced and danced in unity
As laughter filled our childhood dreams
Poo sticks battled swift downstream
Passing 'long reflective skies
We kissed our innocence goodbye

100 Years

In the faraway fields in November
Lay a thousand lost souls in the soil
In mothers cold earth, we remember
As the dead cry of their mortal coil

Clasped by worms in a shrouded existence
As they lie 'mongst the clay and the loam
Haunted heirs of the Devils persistence
Never having the choice to come home

Oh I cry as I ponder your bloodshed
Blindly cut with a gasp and a scream
How I shudder for those who are now dead
Men who's faces I see in my dreams

Let us always remember your fervour
Your ascent into heaven and haze
Clouded images still as a murmur
To remind us the rest of our days

Loves Golden Mile

Look, and ye shall see

For standing, not so far from thee

Is breathlessness

The kind you get, when looking into those eyes

Clear, beautiful pools of lusciousness
Rendering the onlooker, almost unconscious with delirium

Look, and ye shall find
That heart that shines sublime
Along each gilded step, which leads
To the secret garden
Where lovers reign, on a higher plain
Flying freely once again
In wondrous splendour

Oh thou 'doth fill me
Oh love 'doth kill me
With each everlasting kiss
Resounding bliss
And how forever I will remain
Free
Free as part of your conscious spirit

THE LAUGHING BUDDHA & OTHER STORIES

Undying, unifying love

Always

The Woodcock

A dampening of mist

Shrouds the wooded bliss

Half-light in musty melodies

The Woodcock rhoding canopies

Dewy songs arise from steaming bogs

Serenading gently over logs
Lifting verses fly the breeze
As the Woodcock hums amongst the trees

See him not more often than
For colours mix amongst the span
Bark and feather join as one
Until the Woodcock flight 'doth come

The Old Boys of Kentish Town

If you hear a Nightingale, worry for him
As he will sing late, and darkness doth bring vagabonds
Dressed in silken suits, ruffled
Squawking, menacing and gregarious
Laughing if death be hilarious

For these clowns that tread the night air

Will abound in Kentish Square

If you see a rat or two

Worry not

For these black rogues will punish

Whilst spitting sinew between crossed beaks

They will jig to vermin squeaks

To regurgitate cold brains, afore they trickle through the drains

If you hear a midnight chime

Then the sound of crime resonates

Amongst our old boys

Who's lice infested down doth

Bring with it the crown of glory

An untold story of historical myth

Where 'mongst the blackened stone abyss

A cathedral plays home

THE LAUGHING BUDDHA & OTHER STORIES

To the old boys of Kentish Town

In Reflection

I have lived a thousand times
And never felt so alone
My very entity now benign
As I lay me down to drown

And as water passes over me

THE LAUGHING BUDDHA & OTHER STORIES

The view becomes less obscure

My skin is cleansed in purity

My lungs with air that is pure

All doubt recedes beneath the sea

In a slow release

With decades passing furiously

Until I find Peace

Sweet ever lasting Peace

Mountain

And as I trundle, peak bound
Amidst jagged rocks, moss laden
I smell the rose of youthfulness
That reminds me of a maiden

Who loved me so whole heartedly

As clover loves the dew

Beyond the realms of lovers helms

Experienced by few

My mind it wanders far away

To lands of joy and light

Where always I would find her smile

A glowing in the night

Now as I climb above the trees

Among the clouds abound

I hear her voice, soft on the breeze

Where solace can be found

For in my heart she fills the void

Where melancholy dreams

THE LAUGHING BUDDHA & OTHER STORIES

Did once reside, so deep inside

Replaced by lovers screams

The Wood in November

As I step into your mystic world

I foresee peace

I am enveloped in grey

Yet the colours absorb into my body

As if I am a sponge

Oh let me drink more of your inner realms

Quench my emptiness with beauty

Let me walk among old Elms

Linnets and fronds dew bent

Inspire me with sun glints, like swords

Piercing the fern carpets, till bleeding hearts rise

In steamy funnels, canopy bound crows doth cry for immortality

As backdrops colour the scheme with tones of velvet

I am at one with this place

As I walk forever 'mongst it's majesty

In Elders View

In elders view on that summer's eve

When all glee surrounded us

As swallows flourished on mayflies

So sweet as waters glistened in majesty

Heralding her subjects whilst fishermen hum

To the winds ode and wonder

And the trout feel their plunder

Midst the harness of line and hook

Till the sun sets again to embrace sullen stillness

While we meander midst the tawny owls and Ilk

Until a brand new day

The Horsemen

In your futile clamour 'mongst rows of dead

Spew the crows of catatonia clambering overhead

And the murderous gurgles of mortal pith

Resound 'cross the field through scarlet mist
Rich pickings scoured in frenzied greed
As turgid flesh doth fuel the feed
From fletchers hand
To bowmans sight
Consumes the flesh in torrid flight
'till all is gone in hallowed soil
Resounding in deaths eternal coil

Lasting Impression

The fog returns, as daybreak yearns
The dew drops nourishing young ferns
And watercolours brush their way

THE LAUGHING BUDDHA & OTHER STORIES

Across the canvas of today

In mellows of the winter air
Omitting sallow of despair
For ivory black with pthalo green
Obliterates the bleakest scene

Afterthought;
I will walk and wander, till sun subdues
The subtleties of even tide
Leaving only partial views
Impasto, as my soul 'doth glide

September Morning

It was here that I found solitude
On that morning, at the end of summer

Where dew laden berries, plump where sun glows
Glistened midst rose hips in hedgerows

It was here, that I found my spirit
Floating 'mongst daybreaks hues
As fog and lovers' breath
Enveloped my eternal death
And freed me, from my hallowed ground

It was here, youth faded to thought
Only in memory
As years that have travelled, so fast
Find their way.

Back to yesterday

The Edge of Forever

There is a path that leads

THE LAUGHING BUDDHA & OTHER STORIES

To nowhere
Just a few trees and dirt
I sometimes go there

I stand beneath the Judas Tree usually
And ponder
Whilst thinking of the past
No longer

The chalk hills blind me
In whitened gasps
Hares gallop strangely
Amidst Rooks rasps

I hear distant traffic
While standing up here
It doesn't really bother
The Lark or the Deer

THE LAUGHING BUDDHA & OTHER STORIES

I like it here most of the time
Sometimes not
It makes me feel quite sublime
Other days distraught

It's not the place itself
It is within
However I feel
I always return, again and again

Until one day
I won't go back
I'll have done with that place
Forever

The Gilded Wood

Glimmering through hope
Reflecting on leafy memories

Shines loves embrace
Entwining deepest entities

Filling mists with joyous air
Resounding in our ever listening
Comes resolves guiding vapour
'neath canopies of joyous glistening

'Leafy ferns and fervour, breath the everlasting song of nature
Our very own heart, that beats in time
Shimmering in sunlit rapture

Resonance abound, whilst footsteps press the ground
The majesty that all is good
Befitting of this Gilded Wood.

THE LAUGHING BUDDHA & OTHER STORIES

Jenny Wren

THE LAUGHING BUDDHA & OTHER STORIES

Oh colour me in all your glory
As your resonating leaves me high
You tell an unparalleled story
That leaves me with a sweetened sigh

Whilst laying down staring at summer
I'll hear with a whim and a way
Your melody enriched in colours
Of Celandine, Foxglove and May

Hinchelsea Moor

Heather rows and blossom
Spreads it's breath across your view
Catching silken webs in autumn
And the mossy dew

Scots Pine sits in stature
Gazing softly still
In cone flowers and rapture
On a lonely hill

Snipe flit swiftly onward
Passing silent bracken fields
Gorse grows ever upward
Burning as it yields

Summers come and go
In your magic flight and more
In all that you bestow
Across Hinchelsea Moor

The Curlew

Resonate, as Warlocks prose

Curdle in your speckled rows
Amidst a dawn of echoing
In marshes tidal beckoning

Strangling amidst the foggy moors
Riding on the wind and shores
Oh thou haunts thy misty dews
With torrid taunts and whistling mews

Oh Curlew, he who fills thy soul
Whilst heralding a morning stroll
Can fill the silent hum with haze
In these our everlasting days

Winchester Cathedral

THE LAUGHING BUDDHA & OTHER STORIES

Devourer of heresy
In the midst of your realm
Oh Kings would swoon at your feet
With your altar as their helm
'cross oceans in hope and prayer
Your lord did save our souls
Whilst fields of foreign flags and blood
Echo 'mongst your grassy knolls
Gargoyles feast the dusky gnats
'mongst the ghosts and spirits light
Holy Trinity's swathe will feed the bats
And guide us through the eternal night
Stone corbels and dark oak beams abound
Stone facades of Christian piers
Moulded by the Gods resound
Weathered by centuries tears
Still in life as in everlasting death
Bares Aethelwulf 'neath the marbled decks

Effulgent glass in Cromwell's Puritan sway

Upon the altar rage reflects

Behold the bloodied lamb was slain

So Bethlaid's son thrice denied

Your bells do ring in Messiahs name

Oh lord which we abide

Sun in the Morning

My window ajar, I hear Doves calling

Warmth converts my sleepy eyes

To diamonds

That reflect the colours of Provence

Glass omits radiant glows

As I lay, staring throughout

My mouth dry, my heart hungry

As Skylarks resonate the innocence

Fragrance of Honeysuckle clings to my nostrils

Like moths to a flame

As the sun rises higher

To engulf the sandy terrain

Morning is gone

THE LAUGHING BUDDHA & OTHER STORIES

In Sepia Tones

O'er arteries in Alder

Thou morning dancer's gauge

The resolute of nature

'neath sun kissed mornings rage

Coughing, calling splendour

Whilst sparkles light the screams

Go land among the healing hands

Of dewy lain Hornbeams

The Sea

THE LAUGHING BUDDHA & OTHER STORIES

Go back to the sea

Where mortals wash their souls

In time and flesh,

With kindred spills and frothy hills

Herald afresh

Mariners tales,

Of swells and gales

Heraldic sails and Nordic kills

Monsters deep beneath the sputum tide

Breaths aghast amongst monastic glide

Of Poseidon's grasp and Tethys' lair

As sea nymphs clasp and spirits tear

At sailors who would dare to be

The keepers of the harsh cruel sea

Dandelion

Push through the toiled earth in spring

Of magnificence in splendid rays

For warmth to make the Blackbird sing

And fill the everlasting days

The Journeyman

THE LAUGHING BUDDHA & OTHER STORIES

Tread carefully through moonlit snags

October's litter scatterings

How restless rains, cross Salisbury Plain

Relentless windswept battering's

No sheltered moor, or covered shank

Amidst the chalk lain underlings

Hawks bonnets lost, in cosset banks

Beneath where death lies drowning

Fieldfares summon hope in shape, of blood red winter flashes

In turn to fly beneath white skies o'er

Beech and Hawthorns ashes

Tread carefully through the sunlit stilts

Of grassy knolls and loam

'Coz as sure as the Willow wilts

You'll find your way back home

Windswept Jackdaws

THE LAUGHING BUDDHA & OTHER STORIES

Dusky windswept
Blown in circles
Jackdaw's swirl
Flying east, flying west

Calling in flight
As evening is night
Tumbling, turning
Flying north, flying south

Barren trees
To where they flee
To roost amongst it's limbs
Flying east, flying west

Winds do blow
Amongst their huddle
Shaking feathers

THE LAUGHING BUDDHA & OTHER STORIES

Flying north, flying south

Oh Tree

You give up your leaves
To nourish the soil
And lay bare your limbs
Whilst frosts do spoil

Yet naked your branches
Remain for the season
Come spring they will glisten
And give all the reason

To breathe again.

After the Mist

The air is cool but pleasing
As my lungs absorb
To resonate its purity

The Autumn dawn is easing
'mongst the robins 'tick
And sun pierced canopies

Hums of yesterday fill my head
Whilst dreams fulfil
Melodic cacophonies

Eagerly awaited choruses
Of morning Rooks
Haunting melodies

Crawling 'neath my feet
Rippled puddles from

Last eves entities

Till I reach the point
Where all thoughts
Merge with undying, unabridged, distinct purity

Does Love Eternally Be?

Does love eternally be?
In capsicums and white lilies
'mongst Swallowtails and bittersweet
Hiding 'neath thy gliding feet?

Does love eternally be?
For doves whispers, and holly dew
Tall poplars heaven headed
Willow twigs forever threaded

Does love eternally be?
Clouds crying above the sleeping plain
Herald Daisies thirsty for loves rain
In summers golden glimpses

Does love eternally be?
Like bees frequenting meadowsweet
As trembling nettles shy from frost

Till morning brings the yawning mists

Does love eternally be?
Sun kissed poppies in the loam
Kindred spirits heading home
For all eternity
Does Love eternally be?

The Enlightenment

Let's join hips, and chat awhile

Breath while hummingbirds cool our brows

Colouring our eyes with ecstasy while dreaming together

Of intimacy

Let the Deer rub his fur

Gently 'gainst our goosebumps

Watch as his misty breath rises

'twards heaven

And while looking up

Let the leaves gently glide onto our heads

To relieve the sparseness

And shroud us with autumn gold

Let us lay amongst sun kissed daisies

Listening to their sighs

As they point to the sky

For love and strength

And as they open, their sweetness reveals harmony

As Bees nudge their way past our fusion

Creating illusion

In reality

Let the waters immerse us in purity

While Trout whisper sonnets

Heading seawards in rainbows

Oh let the ocean consume our passion

Rolling us over in salty lather

Cleansing our souls

Till we fly deep beneath the sun

Amidst the darkened air

Falling into our journey's end

While kissing sea nymphs

Forever young

The Oystercatcher

Pied imaginings long distant shores
As shells and worms' slide
'neath stones and more

Jewels shimmer deep
Beneath sand lullabies
Awaiting tides return

Eyes scarlet scan the weed
Uncovering molluscs freed
From ebbing tides and windswept tilts
Amidst the Oystercatchers
And sea sewn silt

Down Marks Lane

'tween wood and west

Where's Doves would rest

Cuts old Mark's Lane

'neath Alders pressed

Cajoling through the Yaffles cry

In gravel steps

And Dunnock's sigh

In old Mark's Lane.

The Eve Churr

Be he Moth

Or be he Fly

The Nightjar feasts

In moonlit spry.

The Locust Tree

THE LAUGHING BUDDHA & OTHER STORIES

There is a place
Where Poplars speak
In darkened solace
Of which I seek

There is a place
In moonlit hues
Where I embrace
Alternate views

There is a place
Beyond the realm
Where footsteps trace
The Ancient Elm

There is a place
In which I heal
And where I face

THE LAUGHING BUDDHA & OTHER STORIES

A new ordeal

There is a place
Pure and free
And where I chase
The Locust Tree

Jostling Canopies

Herald the spring, for 'tis time

That feathers fall

And calls do rhyme

'mongst limbs of Fraxinus excelsior

Still leafless

In its rapture

Do the beacons in their fury spew

In Jackdaws grey

And Ravens blue

Hum sorcery amidst the heights

Cajoling through the moonlit flights

Of fancy

And of hunters grasp

Echoing the Rooks course rasps

While country folk do sleep in sheets

The Crows of mirth 'doth guard the sheep.

The Water Meadow

Untouched and surreal
Where I walk
In realms of Marsh Marigolds

Lay memories of past
Where I dream
As the day unfolds

Shimmering sun kissed
Where I lay
'Neath a shady tree

Sonnet filled skies
Where I sleep
For eternity.

The Ecstasy of St. Theresa

(Bernini's Miracle)

Oh Great Lord
Lift up thy useless body
To the divine

As sullen sheets
Do cover my immortality
From the sublime

Oh Holy Spirit
Wash me in your tears
For eternity

As mortals cleanse their souls
From sins
Of uncertainty.

Child of the Earth

Child of the earth
Illuminated by the sun
Our star and guiding light
The glow that shines on everyone

Child of the earth
Your colours glisten in our world
They mingle into one another
As loves is unfurled

Child of the earth
Your smile reaches to afar
Harnessing all gentleness
That shows all that you are

Child of the earth

We are all one, no matter how

Our colours are reflected

To the ones who will allow.......

Their hearts to be open

Their minds to be free

Their love for all others

All wanting to be

The same as each other

No colour or creed

All sisters and brothers

Let our hearts not bleed

Any longer

The Road Ahead

Tread carefully amidst the thistles of tomorrow
Although they can't be seen
For wild as they are, they are full of sorrow
Such underlings will poison your dreams

Move tentatively on with every step
Take heed at the bellowing of night
Breathe in the charged surroundings
Collect your thoughts, be calm, all will be light

Icicles will gather, 'neath your footsteps
Disguised as sheer metallic sunlit jewels
Lift your feet above them 'fore they do meet
As the frosted carpet merges into pools

Thunderous is the night ahead

But sweeten the air it will

The clouds will clear revealing strength

Of nature,

Of love and

Of will......

The Autumn Gathering

As sun descends its solstice tilt
In mystic melodies of lark and snipe
And fore the leaves do fade and wilt
When Autumn sets its flame alight
In ochred minuets once green
Now burgundy and bloods serene
In umbers darkened by the night
Gold gallopings of Hawkmoth's flight
Amidst the serenading chorus of the midday sun
Washed away, as showers smudge the colours into one
And mists arise in awe above your canopies
Revealing hues beyond the realms of glorious majesty.

The Cat

There's a window where I sit
And watch the sheep upon the fields
Grazing peacefully on meadow grass
Bending windward as it yields
There's a window where I sit
As skylarks flock to share their song
Gliding midst the rising hues of gold
And joy all summer long
There's a window where I sit
To see the meadowsweet and hay
Facing sunwards in its glory
Through the merry month of May
There's a window where I sit
As Oaks and Elms begin their plight
Spreading shadows 'neath their majesty
As day turns into night
There's a window where I sit

THE LAUGHING BUDDHA & OTHER STORIES

To find the moon beneath the clouds
Ever changing 'mongst the sprawling
Ever crawling mystic shrouds
There's a window where I sit
As falling leaves show off their skills
Dancing through the windy wilderness
To lay upon the hills
There's a window where I sit
As winters frost begin their hold
Gripping tightly in the hardened earth
As winter tales unfold
There's a window where I sit
As my breath catches the glaze
Misting like the dew before me
To remind me of the days
In the window where I sit

Horsenden Hill

Nestled 'mongst city heights

As tales tell Saxon veils

Swathed in the gilded hum of nestled grasshoppers

Resides her holistic melody as

Sun swept carpets of Bellis in bloom

Do lessen the jettisoned gloom

Of steel birds

To and Fro

And

If one is wise

Then dismiss the fuel filled skies

For heads should ponder

T'wards Harrow and Northolt's Fields

From the beacon that yields

Colour in a monochrome landscape.

Lunar Lament

Your air infuses the heart

Of the sensitive soul

The one who tastes all that is beautiful

In the coldest realms of winter

Your warmth congeals as hope

Your glimpse from heavens clouded shrine

Energy bursting through an entity

Of discourse and doubt

To relieve us all

Oh Moon thou reign greatest

In the night.

The Raven

In your incandescent sheen
And silhouetted flight
'gainst sky and moorland green
Your call beckons the night
Of dark and inky barrows
With shrouded foggy dew
Encased by deathly hallows
Bespoken by The Yew
The hills in which you savage high
And gorge upon the flesh
Resound the haunting lullaby
Of impermanence and death

The Moon (The Shepherd)

A blanket falls upon the high
O'er fields of distant mellow
Drowning in the blackened sky
In mystic hues of yellow
Guiding jostlers to their hides
Amongst the coal lit towers
And elders as they pass besides
The hawthorn tree that cowers
O'er cuckoo spit and flighty stream
As salmon leap their spray
With glow worms heralding their gleam
Through golden orbs of hay

Eternity

Storm clouds will gather

Like galloping horses

Skimming the lands in fury

Whilst farmers tend their flocks

In sodden turf

And maids do turn their locks

In childish mirth

Shutters will hammer their fears

Cajoling angry gods

To disappear

Chimneys screaming as lost souls

Searching for a place to rest

Amidst deaths thunderous rapture

Shuddering trees bow and weep

Roots upturning from the sodden deep

As heavens rain from the abyss

Drench all in fervour, who mortal be

And wash away fragility, to bind us in

Eternity

In Awe of Dusk

Quarter moon

Kissing my spirit in earthly hallows

As rain clouds scream their way

Through semi dark skies

Skeleton trees filtering raindrops

Destined for subterranean mercy

Midst caustic persuasion

From the polluted grind of

Everyday

Morning, noon and night

No respite

THE LAUGHING BUDDHA & OTHER STORIES

On Seeing the Moorland Ghost

Oh joyous sight unto my eye
Your ruddy hide and stature
Your ghost amidst the morning air
In mists of dew and rapture
Breathe amongst the sullen call
Of Cuckoos May time curdle
Whilst Swallows build their clay retreats
And spring streams thunderous burble
Wet footprints in the morning loam
Dug deep intent with pride
Of a Doe's intent to keep herein
The Moorland spirits glide

Printed in Great Britain
by Amazon